Hi! I'm Darcy J. Doyle, Daring Detective,

but you can call me D. J. The only thing better than reading a good mystery is solving one. When spooky noises started coming from Mrs. Pendleton's attic, I had to do something about it. Let me tell you about The Case of the Giggling Ghost.

**Other books in the Darcy J. Doyle,
Daring Detective series:**

Darcy J. Doyle
Daring Detective

The Case of the
Giggling Ghost

Linda Lee Maifair

ZondervanPublishingHouse
Grand Rapids, Michigan

A Division of HarperCollins*Publishers*

The Case of the Giggling Ghost
Copyright © 1993 by Linda Lee Maifair

Requests for information should be addressed to:
Zondervan Publishing House
Grand Rapids, Michigan 49530

Library of Congress Cataloging-in-Publication Data

Maifair, Linda Lee.
    The case of the giggling ghost / Linda Lee Maifair.
        p. cm. — (Darcy J. Doyle, Daring Detective)
    Summary: Darcy Doyle investigates the strange thumping and
scraping noises coming from Mrs. Pendleton's attic.
    ISBN 0-310-57911-2
    [1. Haunted houses—Fiction. 2. Mystery and detective stories.]
I. Title. II. Series: Maifair, Linda Lee. Darcy J. Doyle, Daring
Detective.
PZ7.M2776Cat   1993
[Fic]—dc20   92-39012
                                                            CIP
                                                            AC

Edited by Lori J. Walburg
Interior design by Rachel Hostetter
Illustrations by Tim Davis

Printed in the United States of America

93 94 95 96 97 / ❖ LP / 10 9 8 7 6 5 4 3 2 1

For my mother, with love and gratitude.
Like Mrs. Pendleton,
she is always doing something
for other people.
She has taught me the meaning of love.

CHAPTER 1

I'm Darcy J. Doyle. Some of my friends call me Darcy. Some just call me D.J. If I keep on solving important cases, pretty soon everyone will be calling me Darcy J. Doyle, Daring Detective. It's only a matter of time.

My last big case started at the June meeting of our church's youth service club, the Willing Workers.

"I *hate* washing windows," Mandy Thompson said, making a face at the streaks and smears on the pane of glass in front of her.

"I hope I never see another paint brush," Carol Wilson said. Her hair and clothes were speckled with green.

Greg Sulinski pushed Mrs. Pendleton's sputtering lawn mower to a stop a few feet away. "This must be the lumpiest lawn in Bayside." He rubbed his right shoulder. "I won't be able to lift the bat when we play the Tigers tonight. Whose idea was this anyway?"

I was annoyed when everybody glared at me. After all, Mrs. Pendleton was always doing things for other people. Since she'd broken her hip she couldn't get around very well. I thought it might be nice to do something for her for a change. I was beginning to wonder why we called ourselves the *Willing* Workers. "Oh, it's not that bad," I told them.

Nick Rinaldi stopped hacking at the overgrown hedges in front of the porch. "Not compared to *next* week," he said. "Now *that* will really be bad."

We were supposed to help Mrs. Pendleton inside the house the following Saturday. Dusting, sweeping, mopping, hauling junk out of the

8

attic and cellar. Whatever odd jobs and errands she wanted done. "It's just a little house cleaning," I told Nick. "How horrible can that be?"

"Pretty horrible ..." He paused for effect. "... if the house you're cleaning happens to be *haunted*."

I didn't believe the stories about the old Pendleton place. Just because the house was old and a little run-down didn't mean it was haunted. Mrs. Pendleton liked to have me and my faithful bloodhound, Max, over for cookies and milk now and then. I'd never seen any ghosts. "It's just a bunch of silly rumors," I told Nick. The others didn't think so.

"I'm not going to clean a haunted house," Carol said.

"Me neither," Greg agreed.

"It's not haunted!" I insisted.

"Too bad we can't find out for sure," Mandy said.

"Maybe we can." Nick smiled a strange sort

of smile that made me wonder what he was up to. "How much do you charge, Darcy?"

At first, I didn't know what he was talking about. "For what?"

"To take a case. You know, Darcy Doyle, Darling Detective."

I gave him one of my looks. "That's *daring* detective. And the charge is two dollars . . ." I reminded myself to add a note in my notebook when I got home: *Know-it-all boys, fifty-cents extra.* ". . . and fifty cents."

Nick fished in his pocket and pulled out a rubber band, a gum wrapper, and a crinkled dollar bill. "Here," he said. "I'll pay you the rest when you've finished proving whether or not the house is haunted."

There was a new mystery book I wanted and the dollar looked tempting, but I didn't like the gleam in his eye. "How do you expect me to do that?" I said.

"Well, you could spend the night here with

Mrs. Pendleton . . ." Nick grinned. "And see what happens."

I hesitated. "I don't know if I could . . ."

Nick shook his head at me. "Some *daring* detective you are!" He started to put the dollar back in his pocket.

"Don't bother putting that away," I said. "If Mrs. Pendleton and my folks say it's okay to stay the night, I'll take the case."

Daring Detective or not, I was really sort of disappointed when Mom and Mrs. Pendleton said yes.

CHAPTER 2

My family ate lunch at the Burger Palace.

I swirled a french fry in a blob of ketchup and took my time eating it. "I think Allen should go with me tonight," I said.

My brother nearly choked on his double cheeseburger. My parents exchanged surprised glances. "You *do*?" they said at the same time.

Allen eyed me suspiciously as he swallowed a big wad of sandwich. "Why?" he wanted to know.

I tried to sound as if it really didn't matter to me one way or the other. "Mrs. Pendleton says she never gets any company. She even said we could bring Max. We're going to make taffy." Max and the taffy had been my idea.

Allen licked his lips. "Oh, boy! Taffy!" He gave Dad a pleading, angelic look. "Can I go?"

Dad wasn't quite convinced. "You *want* your brother to go along?" he asked me.

It wasn't that I wanted *Allen*. I just wanted *somebody*. All the other kids had said no. Even Nick Rinaldi. "I have to go visit a sick friend," he'd told me. "Over in Lakemont." A likely excuse.

I sighed as if Allen hadn't been my idea, too. "Mrs. Pendleton thinks he's cute," I said.

Trying to show just how cute he could be, Allen grinned at Mom. "Can I go with Darcy?"

"And good old Max?" I smiled sweetly. I even put a friendly hand on Allen's shoulder. I could be real cute myself when I wanted to.

Mom sighed. "Poor Mrs. Pendleton doesn't know what she's in for."

Allen was ready before I was. We'd only been

home about five minutes when he came into my room, a bulging backpack slung over one shoulder. He watched me stuff my notebook, flashlight, and camera into my gym bag. "What's all that for?" he asked.

I knew he'd keep bugging me until I told him. "I'm on a case," I said.

He made a sour face. "What is it this time?" he asked. "Somebody steal Mrs. Pendleton's string collection?"

I should have kept my mouth shut, but I was annoyed. Hadn't I helped him out by solving the Case of the Mixed-Up Monsters? "No!" I snapped. "Nobody took her string collection or her button jar either. Nick Rinaldi is paying me to find out if the old Pendleton place is haunted."

He thought it over. "Why would anybody think it's haunted?" he asked.

I tried to sound real casual. "Oh, you know. It's big and sort of gloomy looking. People just like to make up stories about ghosts and—" I stopped. There was no sense giving Allen ideas. Besides, I wasn't making myself feel any better.

Allen's face turned pale. "Ghosts?"

I laughed, but the laugh came out sort of high and squeaky. "It's just a bunch of silly stories, Allen. All we have to do is spend the night and—"

Sometimes Allen's smarter than he acts. "So that's why you wanted me to come with you! You're afraid to go by yourself!" He laughed so hard he had to wipe the tears from his eyes.

I didn't slug him. "I'm not afraid," I said. "I just need an assistant."

"Assistant?" I had his interest. "Does this job pay anything?"

Wasn't it bad enough I had to take him at all? "All the taffy you want," I said.

It wasn't enough. "Does Mrs. Pendleton know about this case of yours?" he asked.

I wondered why Mrs. Pendleton thought

Allen was so cute. I hated to do it, but I had no choice. "All the taffy you can eat plus fifty cents?" I offered.

"What if Mrs. Pendleton doesn't want you snooping around her house?" Allen asked me.

"I do *not* snoop!" I told him. "I investigate important cases."

17

Allen can drive a hard bargain when he wants to. We finally settled on a dollar. In advance. I gave him Nick's wrinkled dollar bill. "But you have to do what I tell you," I warned him, "or I get the dollar back."

A half hour later Allen, Max, and I were standing on Mrs. Pendleton's front porch waving at my father as he pulled away in the station wagon.

Mrs. Pendleton motioned us into the house. "I haven't had company for dinner in so long!" It made me feel sort of guilty for not telling her about the case I was working on.

She smiled as if she were really glad we were there. "I thought we'd have fried chicken. And biscuits. As soon as the Sheridan boy gets here with my groceries."

We were having cookies and milk in the parlor when Todd Sheridan arrived, a bag of groceries in each arm. Mrs. Pendleton gave him a chocolate chip cookie to munch on while she went to get the grocery money.

Todd scowled at me. "Weren't you here this morning? Painting and cleaning up the yard?"

I nodded. "The Willing Workers. It's our youth group service project for the month."

Todd helped himself to another cookie from the platter, keeping an eye on Max, who grumbled a little when the cookie went by. "What's wrong with the mutt?" he asked me.

"That's my faithful bloodhound, Max," I told him. "He helps me solve mysteries. He's a trained attack animal."

Todd laughed. "Yeah, sure." He glanced at his watch. "What's keeping her so long?"

He looked around the cluttered sitting room. "My father says somebody should tear this place down, not try to fix it up. Says it ruins the value of the other houses in the neighborhood." He took another cookie.

Good old Max grumbled again, louder. He was as insulted as I was. "Mrs. Pendleton loves this house!" I told Todd. "Her family has lived here for more than a hundred years."

"All I know is my father would like to buy this place and tear down the house. Put in something more useful . . . like a swimming pool." Todd wiped the cookie crumbs on his jeans. "But old lady Pendleton won't sell."

Allen glanced at me, then back at Todd. "Have you ever heard that the house is . . . haunted?" Allen asked.

Todd chuckled at the question. "Wouldn't surprise me a bit!"

"What nonsense!" Mrs. Pendleton said. She was standing in the doorway, the grocery money in her hand. "If this house was haunted, I'd be the first to know it. And I'd never stay in a haunted house!" She held out the money for Todd. "Would you?" she asked him.

He gave her the same sort of smile Nick Rinaldi had given me. "Nobody would do that, Mrs. P.," he said.

CHAPTER 3

We pulled and tugged at the taffy, stretching it out, twisting it around, folding it over, and pulling it out again. Just the smell of it made my mouth water.

I thought I'd do a little Daring Detective work while Allen and Mrs. Pendleton cut it into squares. I washed the butter off my hands and took out my notebook. "Do you mind if I ask you some questions, Mrs. Pendleton?" I said. "For sort of a report I'm doing?"

Allen stuffed a piece of warm taffy in his mouth and talked around it. "Shesh wothin on a big cashe. To shee ish thish housh ish—"

I gave him one of my looks and handed him

another piece of candy, hoping it would glue his mouth shut. "Don't talk with your mouth full, Allen!" My warning had nothing to do with good manners. I smiled at Mrs. Pendleton. "How long have you lived here?" I asked.

"All my life," she said. "Seventy-nine years."

Allen's eyes got real big, as if he thought seventy-nine was really ancient. I handed him another piece of taffy before he could say something dumb. "Have you ever seen anything . . . unusual?" I asked Mrs. Pendleton.

Mrs. Pendleton would make a good Daring Detective. She gave me the sort of smile Mom gives me when she knows exactly what I'm up to. "Like ghosts?" she said.

I could feel my face turn red. "Well . . . uh . . ."

Mrs. Pendleton wiped her hands on her apron. "Darcy, if there had been any ghosts in this house, don't you think I would have seen them by now?"

Allen ran out of taffy. "Ghosts are invisible,"

he said. "Just because you haven't seen them doesn't mean they're not here."

I hated to admit it, but he actually made sense. "Have you ever heard anything unusual, Mrs. Pendleton?" I asked.

She shook her head. "Not a screech or a howl."

I was just writing *no noises, seen no ghosts* in my notebook when the scratching started. A loud, scraping, spooky sort of scratching.

Mrs. Pendleton tilted her head to one side as if she were trying to hear it better. "What on earth . . . ?"

Scraaatch. Scraaatch. Lying on the carpet by the sink, Max opened one sleepy eye.

Scratch, scratch. Scratch, scratch, scratch. Faster and louder than before. Allen stopped right in the middle of popping another piece of taffy into his mouth. "Darcy!" he said.

I cleared my throat. "It's coming from upstairs."

"You're the Daring Detective," Allen said. "Maybe you should go see what it is. I'll just stay here . . . and protect Mrs. Pendleton."

"If I go, you go, Allen Doyle," I said. "You're getting paid to be my assistant, remember?" Neither of us made a move toward the stairway.

"Oh, it's probably just mice . . . or squirrels," Mrs. Pendleton said. "Or a tree branch. Or . . ." She ran out of ideas. "Or something." It was the *something* that had me worried.

Allen too. "Yeah," he said. "Something big and hairy and mean, with big teeth and claws and—"

"Allen!" I whapped him with my notebook. "Will you—"

The scratching stopped. We all smiled. Then we heard something worse than scratching. First came the sound of something big and heavy being dragged across the floor. Then came the weirdest, high-pitched, giggling laughter I'd ever heard. Max opened both eyes.

24

Bump. Thump. Giggle. Giggle. Bang. I tried not to think about what it might be. Unfortunately, Daring Detectives have very good imaginations.

Giggle. Giggle. Bang. Clunk. Giggle. Giggle. Thud.

Max jumped up from his carpet, ran under the table, and put his head in my lap. Good old Max, always ready to protect me.

After two or three minutes of knocking, thudding, banging, and giggling, the noises stopped. The four of us—Allen, Mrs. Pendleton, Max, and I—sat there, holding our breaths. Except for the ticking of Mrs. Pendleton's old wooden wall clock, there wasn't a sound.

I cleared my throat, twice, before I could talk. "I don't think that was a mouse or squirrel, Mrs. Pendleton." I sort of wished she'd come up with a better explanation.

She didn't. "Strange. Very strange," she admitted.

Allen looked a little green, and I don't think it was from all the taffy he'd eaten. He took Nick Rinaldi's crumpled dollar bill out of his pocket and handed it to me across the table. "I want to go home, Darcy," he said.

CHAPTER 4

It's hard to talk somebody into staying in a house he thinks might be haunted . . . especially when you aren't too sure you want to stay there yourself.

"The noise has stopped, Allen," I tried. If he went home now, I'd have to tell Dad the whole story. That would be the end of my case and my two dollars and fifty cents from Nick Rinaldi. Besides, Daring Detectives don't like to give up just when a case gets interesting. "Whatever it was is gone."

Allen didn't buy it. "Maybe whatever it was is just resting. Waiting to jump out and—"

I didn't want to hear it. If he kept that up, I'd be calling Dad myself. I was desperate. "I'll give you an extra fifty cents just to go up to the attic with me. You don't even have to go in. Just stay by the door while I look around a little." I pushed the dollar back across the table.

He picked up the money and stuffed it back into his pocket. "I want the fifty cents in advance, too," he demanded.

I couldn't believe it. "That's all Nick gave me!" I would have slugged him, but Mrs. Pendleton was sitting right there at the table, having a cup of tea. Nice old ladies aren't used to having kids bop each other at the kitchen table. "I'm giving you more than half the money for this case, Allen Doyle, and you don't trust me for it?"

Allen can be real stubborn at times. He crossed his arms over his chest and shook his head. "No fifty cents, no deal."

I can be real stubborn, too. I crossed my

28

hands over my chest, and we sat there glaring at one another.

Mrs. Pendleton got up and went to a cracker tin on the counter. She clinked around with her hand inside the tin and came out with four quarters. She gave two to Allen and two to me. "There," she said. "That settles it."

It made me feel guilty again. "You don't have to pay us anything, Mrs. Pendleton," I said.

"I certainly do," she said. "I'm hiring Darcy Doyle . . . What is it you call yourself, dear?"

I sighed. Why couldn't anybody remember it? "*Daring* Detective," I said.

"I am hiring Darcy Doyle, Daring Detective"—she patted Allen on the hand—"and her able assistant to go check out the attic."

Allen looked at me. I looked at Allen. There was no way around it now. Darcy Doyle, Daring Detective . . . and her *annoying* assistant . . . would have to go to the attic. But I couldn't take Mrs. Pendleton's money. I gave her back the fifty cents. "Thanks, Mrs. Pendleton, but I'm already being paid. By another client."

I gave Allen one of my looks. He didn't act real enthusiastic about it, but he handed her his quarters, too. "And Darcy's already paying me." He looked me in the eye, stubbornly. "A dollar and fifty cents."

"Okay, okay," I said. "But only when I get my money from Nick." We shook hands on the deal. I hated to do it since his fingers were all sticky with taffy, but I knew it would make Mrs. Pendleton happy. I wiped my hand on my jeans and made a note in my notebook. *No more assistants. Especially brothers.*

I glanced at the kitchen window. It was getting dark out. The sooner we went to the attic and came back the better. I handed Allen my bag. "The assistant carries the equipment ... while the detective and her faithful bloodhound investigate for clues."

I grabbed Max by the collar and dragged him

out from under the table. Faithful bloodhounds can be pretty stubborn, too. I half-pushed, half-pulled him in the direction of the hall stairway.

I stopped to catch my breath in the doorway and gave Mrs. Pendleton what I hoped was a confident smile. "Don't worry, Mrs. Pendleton. The Lord will watch over us. We should be back in a couple of minutes," I told her. Half a minute up the stairs, a minute to look around, and half a minute back. Only two minutes. How bad could it be?

Pretty bad when you have somebody like Allen for an assistant. He trudged up behind me looking like he was on his way to the principal's office. He didn't even try to smile. "*If* we come back at all," he said.

"Where's your faith, Allen Doyle?" I asked him. I reminded myself to ask Pastor Jordan about ghosts after church and started reciting a little of the 23rd Psalm. "The Lord is my shepherd . . ."

Allen interrupted with a question of his own. "Why's your voice shaking like that, Darcy Doyle?" he said.

CHAPTER 5

Mrs. Pendleton had one of those old-fashioned attics full of cardboard cartons, old chests, and worn-out furniture. Sometimes she let me come up and try on old hats and dresses. It was a great place to play in the daytime.

At night, in a house that might be haunted, it didn't look the same. The bare-bulbed light in the center of the room cast weird shadows over everything. The sheet-covered overstuffed chair in the far corner looked like a chubby ghost with wide-open arms.

I whispered a little prayer and forced myself to move forward. Max walked so close he nearly tripped me with every step. Good old Max. Always worried about protecting me. "You look over there," I told Allen. "I'll check out this corner."

He didn't budge from the top step. "You said I didn't have to go in. You said I could just stay by the door while you looked around."

It was a fine time for him to start listening to what *I* had to say. "Some assistant you are," I snapped. "Hand me my flashlight."

I had to walk over to the doorway to get it. With the flashlight in one hand, my notebook in the other, and my pencil stuck behind my ear, I edged toward the darker corners of the room. I flashed the light around the ceiling beams and along the floor.

"What are you looking for?" Allen called from the stairwell.

I had no idea. "Clues," I said. "Don't you know anything?"

"What kind of clues?" he asked.

How did I know what kind of clues I was looking for before I found them? "Something to lead us to the perpetrator," I told him.

"To the perpa . . . *what?*"

I checked out the cardboard cartons scattered around at the far end of the room. "Perpetrator," I said. "Whoever was making all the noise." I was sure the cartons had been stacked up, in a row, the last time I was in the attic. I wrote *boxes moved around* in my notebook.

"Do ghosts leave clues?" Allen wanted to know.

"All perpetrators leave clues," I said. "It's up to us Daring Detectives to find them."

Max was looking as hard as I was. He sniffed his way around the attic, coming to a stop over by the chimney. He yipped and whined and wagged his tail. I ran over to see what had him so excited. He was licking at something on the floor.

"Look at this! Good old Max has found a clue." I held up a soggy candy wrapper. "Ghosts don't eat candy bars." At least I didn't think so.

Allen edged into the room. "Maybe it's Mrs. Pendleton's," he suggested.

"Mrs. Pendleton doesn't eat candy bars either," I made a note of it. "Look for more clues," I told Allen. "Anything unusual."

A few minutes later he held up an old safari type hat. "This is pretty unusual," he said. "It's all bumpy."

It *was* bumpy. Dented in on the top. I got down on my hands and knees and ran the flashlight beam over the floor. "I wonder what made these marks on the floorboards?"

Allen knelt down beside me. "Looks like somebody hit it with a hammer."

I smiled. "Or a hard safari hat."

Allen made a face. "Why would anybody beat a hat against a floor?" he said. "It doesn't make sense."

"No," I agreed. "But it would make a lot of noise." I wrote *dented hat* and *marks on floor* in my notebook. Still on my hands and knees, I found a pair of squiggly skid marks leading to the overstuffed ghost chair. *Chair moved away from other furniture*, I wrote. *Trail to legs.*

"Go down to the kitchen," I told Allen. "See if you hear the same noises you heard before."

I gave him time to get downstairs. I pushed the big overstuffed chair across the room and back to the corner again. Then I banged the dented safari hat against the floor.

Allen came clumping up the stairs two at a time. "It . . . sounded just . . . the same," he said breathlessly.

"I knew it!" Daring Detectives get real excited when we're about to crack a big case. "And I think I know who did it, too."

"You *do?*" Allen looked impressed.

I nodded. "If I could just figure out how he got up here to . . ."

Whine. Whine. Bark. Max was pawing at the window ledge. I went over to pull him back. There was a little chunk of candy bar out on the porch roof. The window was open about two inches, a wedge of wood holding it in place.

"Good old Max!" I gave him a hug. I added *came in window* to my notes. Then I opened the window, picked up the piece of candy, wrapped it in a tissue, and put it in my pocket. Max whined and wagged his tail. He always knows important evidence when he sees it.

"Come on," I told Allen. "I have a phone call to make." Max was as excited as I was. He practically chased me down the stairs.

Nick Rinaldi's mother answered the phone. "Nick just got home," she said.

I smiled. I knew exactly where Nick Rinaldi had been. Up in Mrs. Pendleton's attic making noises, trying to make me think the house was haunted.

"You can't fool Darcy J. Doyle, Daring Detective, Nicholas Rinaldi," I told him when he finally came to the phone.

"Huh?" he said.

"Don't try to act innocent," I warned him. "I have all the evidence I need. The chair. The dented hat. The chocolate bar you were eating."

"You have to be kid—"

"It was a mean trick, Nick. You scared poor Mrs. Pendleton . . . and Allen." He hadn't done me and good old Max much good either, but I didn't tell him that.

"Darcy!" Nick sounded exasperated. "I don't know what you're talking about."

I was annoyed. Now that I'd solved the case, the least he could do was confess to the crime. "I'm talking about you coming here tonight and climbing up Mrs. Pendleton's porch railing and into her attic, making ghost noises and—"

"If you heard noises, Darcy Doyle, I didn't make them," Nick insisted. "In the first place, I'm allergic to chocolate. In the second place, I was with Dad all night. Visiting my cousin Rick in the hospital. Dad's right here if you want to ask him."

I felt sort of sick to my stomach. People don't offer to put their fathers on the phone unless they're telling the truth. "Uh . . . never mind."

"And Darcy?" Nick said.

I had a feeling I knew what he wanted. "Yeah, Nick?"

"You're fired."

CHAPTER 6

"You still owe me the dollar fifty. It's not my fault you got yourself fired," Allen said. He laughed, his mouth full of half-chewed pancakes. It wasn't a very pretty sight. "Accusing your own client!"

"If I'm fired, you're fired, too," I told him. I didn't see why I should pay him if Nick wasn't going to pay me. Being fired, I'd probably have to give Nick back his dollar. Allen was wearing it inside his dirty sock so I couldn't get my hands on it.

"The pancakes are wonderful, Darcy." Mrs. Pendleton held out her plate. "I think I'll have another." I wasn't sure if she was really hungry or just trying to change the subject.

Pancakes were my specialty. I'd learned the secret ingredient—a spoonful of vanilla—at church camp the summer before. I went over to the stove and poured batter onto the griddle.

Mrs. Pendleton took a sip of her tea. "I'd still be willing to pay each of you fifty cents to find out who was fooling around in my attic last night."

I was willing to take the case. If word got around about how I'd bungled things with Nick, people would be calling me Darcy J. Doyle, Dumb Detective. I just wasn't sure I should take the money. I flipped the pancake over on the griddle. "Uh . . ."

Mrs. Pendleton read my mind. "It will be money well spent."

I scooped up the pancake, slid it onto Mrs. Pendleton's plate, and set it down in front of her. "I'll go get my notebook," I said.

Allen was having a mouthful of taffy for dessert when I got back. "Mmmf." He worked the wad to the side of his mouth. "Maybe Nick had somebody else do it?" he suggested. "So he'd have a . . . what do you call it?"

"An alibi?" I'd considered that myself. "I don't think so. Would you go into that attic at night for somebody else?"

Allen grinned. "I already did," he said. "And she still owes me fifty cents."

I ignored the hint. "I think it's somebody else."

Mrs. Pendleton made her way over to the sink and started rinsing syrup off the plates. "Why would anybody want to do such a thing?" she asked. "You poor children were scared to death."

Neither of us would admit it. "He was scared, not me," I said.

"I wasn't scared, she was," Allen said. A rap on the kitchen door interrupted the argument and scared both of us.

Allen walked over and peeked out between the drapes on the door. "It's that grocery kid."

"That's strange," Mrs. Pendleton said. "He never comes without being asked. And this morning his father came over, offering to buy the house again. He said he'd heard I might have changed my mind about selling. I don't know where he'd get such a notion." She motioned to Allen to open the door.

Todd Sheridan stepped into the kitchen. "I'm going down to the store, Mrs. P. You need anything?"

She seemed real surprised that he asked. "Why, no, Todd. I don't believe that I do. Thank you!"

He hesitated, as if there were something on his mind but he didn't want to come right out and say it. He pulled a stick of gum out of his pocket and unwrapped it. He stuck the gum in his mouth, balled up the paper, and stuffed it into his jacket pocket. "Anything new?"

That surprised Mrs. Pendleton, too. "Why, no, Todd. Anything new with you?"

He shook his head. "Nah. Same old thing. Wish there was more to do around here in the summertime." He shoved his fists into his pockets. Something small, round, and shiny fell to the floor at his feet.

He didn't notice, but I did. Daring Detectives are very observant. The pieces began to fit together. "Too bad you don't have that pool you wanted," I said.

He frowned at Mrs. Pendleton as if it were all her fault. "Yeah, too bad."

"You know," I said, trying to sound real cool and casual about it. "We had some excitement over here last night."

Todd looked real interested. "Yeah?"

"There were all these weird noises," Allen said. "Up in the attic. Darcy thought it was one of her friends trying to scare us, but it wasn't. We don't know what it was. Mrs. Pendleton's paying us each fifty cents to—"

I felt like stuffing a sock . . . the one with the dollar in it . . . in his mouth. I interrupted instead. "It was really spooky." I tried to make it real dramatic. "We were all scared silly."

Allen looked like he'd just won the lottery. "I knew you were scared!" he said.

Sometimes I wished he'd go somewhere else . . . like South America. We were studying the animals of South America in Science. Monkeys, big, hairy spiders, pythons, hyenas. I thought

46

Allen would fit right in. "We were all scared," I told Todd. "We think it might be ghosts."

Mrs. Pendleton raised an eyebrow at me. "Why, Darcy, dear, you know very well—"

I hated to do it, but I had to. "Yeah," I interrupted. "I know how you said you'd have to move if there were ghosts in the house." Her mouth sort of fell open, but she didn't say anything. I went on talking. "I hope it doesn't happen again. I sure wouldn't want Mrs. Pendleton to move out. Wouldn't that be awful?" I asked Todd.

He didn't smile so you'd notice it, but the corners of his mouth twitched just a little. "Yeah. Terrible." He glanced at his watch. "I gotta go."

He paused in the doorway. "I don't blame you a bit, Mrs. P. I wouldn't stay if the place was haunted, either. All that bumping and scraping—" He stopped. "Terrible," he repeated. "Just terrible."

As soon as he left, I bent down and picked up

the small shiny object that Todd had dropped without knowing it. I smiled. I'd solved the case. And, this time, I was sure I was right.

"Darcy, dear," Mrs. Pendleton said, putting a hand on my shoulder. "What was all this nonsense about me leaving the house?"

"Yeah," Allen chipped in. "What are you up to now, Darcy Doyle?"

"Todd knew about the bumping and scraping. All you told him was that there were noises." I held out the gum wrapper that had fallen, like the candy wrapper, from Todd's pocket. "I'm not up to anything," I said. "I'm just baiting a trap."

Allen's brow wrinkled in confusion. "A trap? For what?"

Mrs. Pendleton caught on right away. "Not for what, for *whom*, dear," she told Allen. "Darcy's trying to catch our giggling ghost!"

CHAPTER 7

The next night, we were back in Mrs. Pendleton's attic. The plan was simple. So was my number-one assistant. "I can't see a thing!" Allen complained.

That was the whole idea. If we couldn't see each other across the dark attic, Todd Sheridan couldn't see us either. "Shhh," I told Allen.

"This is really boring," Allen grumbled.

"It'll get real exciting when he gets here," I promised.

"You can't even be sure he'll come," Allen muttered.

"He'll come," I said. He had to. How else was

I going to prove that I really was a Daring Detective? "Would you be *quiet*!"

He was quiet for all of five seconds. Crackle. Crackle. Crunch. Crunch. Crunch.

"Allen! Why are you eating potato chips on a stakeout?"

"I'm hungry." Crunch. Crunch. He might as well greet Todd Sheridan with a drum roll.

Even my number-two assistant was annoyed. "Allen Ryan Doyle, put those chips away," Dad ordered. I'd told him all about the giggling ghost and my trap when he picked us up that morning. I was really sort of glad when he'd insisted on coming along.

Crackle. Crackle. Allen tried to sneak another chip.

"*Allen*!" Dad and I said at the same time.

Max decided to take matters into his own paws. Gallump. Gallump. Gallump. He bounded across the room. "Max! Come back here!" I whispered.

"No, Max. Let go!" Allen didn't bother to whisper. "They're mine!"

Crackle. Crackle. Grumble. Growl. Gallump. Gallump. Something big and furry sat back down beside me. Crackle. Crunch. Gobble. Gobble.

"Max stole my bag of chips!" Allen complained.

Dad wasn't very sympathetic. "Good!" he said.

Good old Max wasn't taking any chances with the rest of the chips. He finished them off. He knew how important this case was to me. He wanted to be sure Allen wouldn't tip off the perpetrator with all that noise.

"Just be quiet and try to remember what you're supposed to do," I told Allen.

"If we don't all get quiet, there won't *be* anything to do," Dad reminded us.

I leaned back against Max, shut my eyes, and went over the plan in my mind. Todd would come in the window. He'd start dragging the chair and stuff around. Allen would pull the string we'd attached to the light to turn it on. I'd jump out and take pictures for evidence. And Dad would grab him if he tried to get away. Simple. I was still picturing it in my mind when I heard muffled noises on the roof outside the attic window.

"Darcy!" Allen whispered loud enough for Mrs. Pendleton to hear downstairs in the parlor.

"I know! I know!" What was he going to do next, open the window and ask Todd if he needed a hand?

The skin on the back of my neck got all tingly as I heard the window slide up, slowly. I wiped my sweaty palms on my jeans and got a better grip on my camera.

A small light snapped on. The person holding it made his way over to the safari hat and knelt down on the floor. Bang. Bang. Giggle. Giggle. Bang.

52

He got up and stomped across the attic to the cardboard cartons. Thump. Thud. Giggle. Giggle. Thump. He picked them up one at a time and dropped them on the floor.

He went over to the big, overstuffed chair, set the flashlight down on the seat cushion, and started pulling the chair across the room. Scraaaape. Scraaaape. Giggle.

That was Allen's signal to turn on the light. I stood up, my finger on the snap button of the camera, but no light came on. The person stopped dragging and pushing the chair. He picked up his flashlight and headed toward the window.

"Turn on the light, Allen!" I yelled.

Allen gave a mighty tug on the light cord. Too mighty. The light flickered on then right back off as the cord broke in his hand.

The culprit bolted toward the window. Dad came running out from behind a pile of boxes. "Get him, Dad!" I yelled. I gave Max a shove toward the middle of the room. "Go sit on him, Max!" Good old Max charged across the room with me right behind him.

"Ooof!"

"Ouch!"

"Woof!"

"Look out!"

Thud. Thump. We all ended up in a heap in the middle of the room. An elbow poked me in the ribs. Flash. Flash. Flash. The camera went off several times.

"Get off me, you dumb dog!" Allen groaned in a squashed sort of voice.

"Darcy!" Dad sounded sort of exasperated. "Quit flashing that thing in my eyes!"

"I've got him, Dad!" I shouted. "I've got him!" I set the camera down and wrapped the broken light cord around the pair of legs I was sitting on. I knotted the cord three times, then wrapped it around tightly and knotted it again.

The culprit laughed loudly from the other

side of the room. I didn't have time to wonder whose legs I'd been tying together. I couldn't let Todd get away. "Cookies, Max!" I yelled. "He's got cookies!"

Max got off of Allen and charged toward the window. In the dim, bouncing glow of Todd's flashlight, I could make out a little of the struggle. Todd tried to pull himself through. Max caught him by the sneaker and wouldn't let go. Max was real stubborn when cookies were involved.

"Let go of me, you stupid mutt!"

Grrrrrr. Grrrrrr. Grrrrrrr.

"The light, Dad!" I yelled. He was the only one who could reach it with the broken cord. "Turn on the light!" I found my camera by tripping over it. I picked it up and ran toward the window. "He's going to get away!" I shouted.

My assistants were having their own troubles.

"Allen, let go of my leg!"

"I can't, Dad."

"Where *is* that light cord? Ow!"

"Oops. Sorry, Dad."

Snap! Snap! The camera flash went off in my eyes. All I could see were big yellow dots.

When the dots cleared a little, I could see Max having a tug of war with a sneaker. Max was on the inside of Mrs. Pendleton's attic window, his teeth clenched around the heel of the shoe. Todd was out on the window ledge trying to pull his foot free.

Todd Sheridan was smarter than I thought. He reached down and untied the sneaker. The shoe came off and Max fell over backwards into the room.

"He's getting away!" I shouted again.

My assistants were still too busy to notice.

"Allen, that's my foot you keep stomping on."

"I can cut the cord with my scout knife, Dad."

"Not in the dark you can't, Allen."

"Maybe if we sit down it'll be easier."

Whine. Whine. Howwwlll!

I started making my way toward the attic door, feeling the wall for the light switch as I went. Somebody beat me to it. The light clicked on.

"My goodness!" Mrs. Pendleton said. She had this really strange look on her face . . . as if she was trying hard not to laugh.

I could see why. Max was leaning out the attic window howling at the culprit who'd run off with the cookies. Dad and Allen were sitting together in the middle of the floor, trying to undo the light cord I'd used to tie their legs together. And Darcy J. Doyle, Daring Detective, had let the giggling ghost get away.

CHAPTER 8

Dad tried to make me feel better. "It's not so bad, Darcy," he said.

"It's terrible!" I told him. "None of us got a good look at Todd. We didn't catch him in the act. And he'll never be dumb enough to come back so we can try again."

Mrs. Pendleton patted me on the shoulder. It's okay, dear. Todd won't be bothering me anymore. That's all that matters."

That did matter. But it wasn't all that mattered. Daring Detectives can be as stubborn as faithful bloodhounds who think someone's taken their cookies. Darcy J. Doyle doesn't like leaving a case unsolved. "He shouldn't just get away with it," I said.

"You're right, Darcy," Dad agreed. He reached across the table for my camera. "First thing in the morning we'll take this roll of film down to Super-Photo. Maybe you got some evidence after all."

We dropped off the film at 9:00 a.m. and picked up the pictures an hour later. Except for a couple of really embarrassing close-ups of Dad and myself, only one of them turned out very well.

Allen made a face. "You can't use that, Darcy."

I was annoyed. I had to use it. It was all I had. Other than a chewed-up sneaker and a chunk of chocolate that had melted all over the inside of my shirt pocket, it was just our word against Todd Sheridan's.

"Oh, yes, I can," I said. "If you and Dad and Mrs. Pendleton will help me."

Dad raised an eyebrow. "What do you expect me to do now?"

I told him the plan. An hour later we were back in Mrs. Pendleton's kitchen waiting for Todd Sheridan. Todd didn't look very happy to see my father sitting at the table.

"Whatever they told you, it isn't true," he said.

Dad smiled. "They've got proof, Todd."

"What proof?" Todd demanded.

I showed him the candy wrapper. "Lots of people eat those," he said.

I held up the tattered sneaker. "I'll bet we could find the match to this over at your house," I said.

He smiled. "I bet you couldn't."

I hadn't counted on him throwing away the sneaker. It sort of took me by surprise. Todd laughed. "You can't prove anything."

"We saw you," I told him. "Dad, too."

"Todd shook his head. "You couldn't have

seen anything. It was too . . ." He stopped. "I'm leaving!" he said. He put his hand on the doorknob.

"It was too what, Todd? Too dark?" I asked him. "How would you know that, unless you were there?"

"You said it was up in the attic . . . at night. Anybody could guess that it was dark," he said. "You've got no real proof and you know it." He turned the knob.

"Show him the picture, Dad," I said.

Todd spun around. "You couldn't have gotten a good picture," he said.

Dad took a photo out of his pocket. He held it up. "Actually, it's a very good picture," he said. "Looks just like him, doesn't it, Mrs. Pendleton?"

Mrs. Pendleton nodded at the photo. "No question at all who it is." Todd's face turned pale. Dad should have been an actor. He held the photograph out toward Todd and smiled a broad smile. "Care to see it, Todd?"

I held my breath, hoping that Todd would feel the same way I had when Nick asked if I wanted to talk to his father. He shook his head. "What are you going to do about it?" he asked.

"Let's turn him in to the police!" Allen suggested. Todd looked a little green.

"Let's just take the picture over and show his folks," I said. Todd looked even greener.

"Of course, if you did something to show how sorry you are for trying to scare Mrs. Pendleton," Dad told Todd, "I could put in a good word with your folks."

Todd brightened a little. "What do you want me to do?" he said.

Dad's a lot like Allen when it comes to driving a hard bargain. When it was all over, Todd had "volunteered" to take care of Mrs. Pendleton's yard work the rest of the summer.

"He did want something to do," Allen told Dad when Todd had gone.

"Well, that should keep him out of trouble."

Dad grinned at the photograph. "It really *is* a good picture, Darcy." He handed me the snapshot.

Mrs. Pendleton went over to her cracker tin and fished out four quarters. She gave two to Allen and two to me. I thanked her and put the money and the picture in my pocket.

After I paid Nick Rinaldi back his dollar, the case only ended up costing me fifty cents. But that was okay. After all, I had a really great picture of good old Max to put in my notebook of Important Cases Solved by Darcy J. Doyle, Daring Detective.